Kita
and the
Magic Paint

By Laura Schaumer

Illustrated By Pardeep Mehra

www.lauraschaumerbooks.com

ISBN: 978-1-7774534-2-8 (HardBack)
        978-1-7774534-1-1 (PaperBack)
        978-1-7774534-0-4 (eBook)
        978-1-7774534-3-5 (Coloring Book)
        978-1-7774534-4-2 (French Edition)

Dedicated to my daughter,
Madison
who shows me that there
is magic in everything you do.

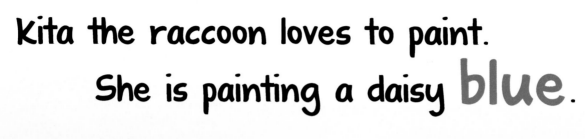

Kita the raccoon loves to paint.
She is painting a daisy **blue**.

Bushy the squirrel loves
to paint, too. He is
painting a daisy red.

Kita wants her flower to be **red** and **blue**. She has an idea. "Let's swap paint cans," she says.

Kita puts red paint on her blue daisy.

Bushy puts blue paint on his red daisy. "My daisy is turning purple too," he squeals.

"How did the colors change?" asks Kita.
"It must be magic," says Bushy.

"Let's try other colors," says Kita.
Now Kita paints a daisy yellow.
Bushy paints a daisy blue.

The friends swap paint cans again. Kita puts blue paint on her yellow daisy.

"It turned green," she squeals.

Bushy puts yellow paint
on his blue daisy.

"Mine turned green, too," he yells.
"This is magic!" shouts Kita.
"Amazing!" says Bushy.

Artie the monkey comes to see why his friends are so excited. "Artie, we have Magic paint!" shouts Kita.

"Watch this," says Kita.
This time she paints
a daisy red.

Bushy paints a daisy yellow.
Artie watches as they swap paints.
Kita puts yellow paint on her red daisy.

"It turned **orange**!" says Artie.

Bushy puts red paint
on his yellow daisy.

"Yours is turning orange, too," Artie says.

All the friends gather to watch the colors change. Now they all want to paint. Each friend brushes paint on a daisy.

Annie the Bunny is hopping along...

and then....

She lands right on top of the painted daisies. Annie looks silly. Everyone laughs.

She hop, hop, hops on the grass...

"Now we have rainbow footprints and rainbow flowers," says Kita.

Magic paint is so much fun!

About the Author

Laura graduated from George Brown with a Certificate in American Sign Language. Along with her educational background, she is an avid writer who fully understands how to communicate with children. Laura is a devoted mother of one and is married to her loving husband, Daniel. Laura loves spending her early mornings writing with a big cup of coffee. She lives in Ontario enjoys camping, listening to live concert music and doing arts and crafts. She is currently working on her next book, to be out in 2021. Visit www.lauraschaumerbooks.com.

About the Illustrator

Pardeep Mehra is the founder of Pencil Master Digital Studio, a family-owned business employing a large group of talented artists providing end to end illustration and publishing services.

For more than 15 years, Pardeep has been providing his keen eye, visualization and digital art skills to create hundreds of beautifully illustrated books that delight children all over the world. Pardeep lives in India with his wife Priyam and daughter Mehar. For more info and portfolio review, visit www.pencilmasterdigi.com.

Color your own daisy.

Made in the USA
Monee, IL
19 June 2021